Ron

Rudi's Birthday Extravaganza

written and illustrated by

Maxine Sylvester

★ I ★

To
Pat, Den and Bren

Copyright © 2019 Maxine Sylvester

The moral right of the author has been asserted.
Apart from any fair dealing for the purposes of research or private study,
or criticism or review, as permitted under the Copyright, Designs and Patents
Act 1988, this publication may only be reproduced, stored or transmitted, in
any form or by any means, with the prior permission in writing of the
publishers, or in the case of reprographic reproduction in accordance with
the terms of licences issued by the Copyright Licensing Agency. Enquiries
concerning reproduction outside those terms should be sent to the publishers.

Contents

1. Rudi's Hoof   1
2. Doctor Kloppen's Humungous Needle   11
3. Mrs Sorrenson's Scrumptious Carrot Cake   22
4. The Mysterious Doe with the Shopping Bags   30
5. Wind, Wind and More Wind!   38
6. The Vixen Pederson Interview   50
7. The End of Term Exam   60
8. Grumpy Ronny   72
9. The Mrs Sorrenson Cake Incident   76
10. Mr Gunnersson's Babas   83
11. *FrizzNo* Fever!   90
12. The Reindeer Flyover   96
13. Mrs Sorrenson's Apprentice   110
14. An Unexpected Encounter   118
15. Rudi's Near-Disastrous Birthday Party!   125
16. Monty the Moose?   132
17. Monty Unmasked   138
18. Rudi's Birthday Extravaganza   145

Chapter One

Rudi's Hoof

"Twenty-seven, twenty-eight, twenty-nine, thirty!" Ronaldo patted his hooves together with excitement. He had enough money to buy his best friend, Rudi, a pair of flying goggles. His birthday was in a few weeks and Ronaldo wanted to get him something special. He flicked through the FLY-X catalogue.

Should I buy banana-yellow

or luminous lime?

He grabbed his ice cold carrotade and finished it in one gulp. "Phew!" On hot days like this, he wished he didn't have a fur coat. At least the heat hadn't made his hair go frizzy – unlike his dad, who, like many of the grown-up reindeer, resembled a windswept poodle! Ronaldo giggled just thinking about him.

Bang, bang, bang!

He rushed to the bedroom window to see who was knocking on the front door. But whoever it was had already gone inside.

"Ronaldo!" Dad called from downstairs.

Ronaldo padded on to the landing and peered over the bannister.

Dad was ushering Mrs Gunnersson, Rudi's mother, into

the hallway. She had a grey face with white freckles splattered across her nose, just like Rudi did.

And crikey, she had a terrible case of the frizzies! Her hair made Dad's look quite fashionable.

"Oh, Ronaldo!" she ran her hoof through her crazy mane. "It's Rudi!"

"Is it his front hoof?" Ronaldo remembered his friend catapulting over a tree stump on roller skates the previous day.

"It's swollen," she wailed. "I've made an appointment to see Doctor Kloppen today."

"*Oh!*" Ronaldo took a step back from the bannister.

"Oh, indeed." Mrs Gunnersson sighed. "You know what Rudi's like. Terrified of needles! He's locked himself in his bedroom and he won't come out."

She looked up at Ronaldo, her eyes the colour of blueberry jam. "Maybe you could

have a word with him? And come with us to see Doctor Kloppen?"

Ronaldo stood there, unsure what to say. He didn't like Doctor Kloppen any more than Rudi did. But then again, the doctor did have a huge jar of lollipops on his desk. The carrot and lemon ones were particularly scrumptious.

"Sure, no problem," he said, smiling.

Ronaldo trotted through the woods with Mrs Gunnersson. The hot weather had melted the snow. Dandelions dotted the blanket of luscious green grass.

"Oh, this heat!" Mrs Gunnersson wiped beads of sweat from her forehead.

"I really miss snow," Ronaldo grumbled. "I don't think reindeer are meant to roller skate. We're far better at sledging."

The Gunnerssons' home had bright yellow walls and a turquoise rooftop. White painted daisies decorated the front door and baskets loaded with colourful flowers hung on either side of the doorframe. Ronaldo thought the house looked fun and cheerful, a bit like Rudi himself.

"Go on up," Mrs Gunnersson said.

Ronaldo took the stairs two at a time. He knocked on Rudi's bedroom door.

"Rudeee. It's me."

"Hi, Ronny," said a muffled voice from the other side of the door. "I'm glad you're here. I can give you this."

Swoosh! A luminous pink envelope, decorated with glittery purple stars, appeared under the door.

Ronaldo sat down on the floor and picked up the envelope with interest.

"It's an invitation to my birthday party," Rudi said.

Ronaldo frowned. Rudi had ruined the surprise.

"And guess what?"

"What?"

"Monty the Moose is coming!"

"Monty the Moose!" Ronaldo's face lit up like a firefly's bum. Monty was the most fantastic magician in the whole world! Ronaldo never missed

his Wednesday night television show.

"Mum and Dad have already booked him."

"That's awesome!" Ronaldo squealed.

"Ahem."

Ronaldo nearly jumped out of his fur. He hadn't heard Rudi's mum creep up behind him.

"So, umm, how's your hoof, Rudi?" he said, smiling up at Mrs Gunnersson.

"It's really sore. Last time I'm roller skating."

"Me too!" Ronaldo said, staring at his grazed knees.

Mrs Gunnersson pointed to her watch. "Please hurry, Ronaldo," she whispered. "His appointment's in half an hour."

Ronaldo nodded. "Maybe you should

see Doctor Kloppen, Rudi?" he winced at the sound of his name.

"No way!" Rudi growled.

Mrs Gunnersson looked down at Ronaldo, her arms folded over her chest. Ronaldo stared at her fuzzy hair, mesmerised. He shook his head. *Focus Ronny!*

Aha! He had an idea.

"It's the end of term Reindeer Flyover next week," he said. "Wing Commander Blitsen won't let you fly with an injured hoof."

Ronaldo smiled smugly. There's no way Rudi would want to miss out on such a historical event.

Mrs Gunnersson nodded her head in approval.

"But Doctor Kloppen might use his needle. It's HUMUNGOUS, Ronny!" Rudi's voice rose in fear.

"Maybe he'll just give you medicine... and he's got lollipops to take away the nasty taste," Ronaldo said.

"Hmmm," Rudi sighed.

Tap, tap, tap! Mrs Gunnersson pointed to her watch again.

"Is my mum there?" Rudi said, his voice gruff.

"No! Just me." Ronaldo frowned. He hated lying to Rudi.

Mrs Gunnersson sneaked away into the bathroom.

Click!

The bedroom door opened and Rudi crept out.

Woah! Ronaldo's eyes nearly popped out of his head. Rudi's hoof was the size of a beluga whale!

"Hello, Ronaldo," Mrs

Gunnersson said, as she casually stepped out of the bathroom.

"Oh, hi," Ronaldo said, feigning surprise.

"Rudi and I are off to see the doctor. Would you like to come with us?"

Rudi held up his whale-sized hoof. "Pleeeeeeeease!"

Ronaldo pictured brightly coloured lollipops. He grinned. "Okay," he said.

Chapter Two

Doctor Kloppen's Humungous Needle

Ronaldo and Rudi stopped in the centre of Beresford.

"I've never seen the village so quiet," Ronaldo said.

"It's sweltering," Rudi moaned. "Maybe everyone's down at the lake?"

"Stop dawdling," Mrs Gunnersson called over her shoulder. "We're gonna be late."

Ronaldo and Rudi followed her down a narrow side street.

"Mmmmmm." They lifted their noses. The 'Carrots 'N' Cakes' bakery! The two fawns trotted like zombies, then hovered outside the bakery window.

Every cake imaginable was crammed on to the left side of the display case. From carrot and chocolate éclairs to carrot and jam twirly-whirlies, carrot and toffee slices to carrot and raspberry sponges. And the right-hand side looked even more delectable. A sign at the top read: *Mrs Sorrenson's Scrumptious Sweets*.

"I *love* Mrs Sorrenson's cakes," Ronaldo drooled. "My parents have all her baking books."

"Her carrot cake's really famous," Rudi

said, in awe. "Look at the size of it."

They gazed at the enormous cake slathered in cream. It was decorated with orange sprinkles and mounted upon a pyramid of carrot and strawberry cupcakes.

"RUDOLPH GUNNERSSON!"

Ronaldo and Rudi's fur stood on end. An angry Mrs Gunnersson, complete with fuzz-ball hair, marched towards them.

"I'm off!" Rudi charged towards the doctor's surgery before his mum had a chance to catch him.

"Sorry we're late," Mrs Gunnersson panted, as the three reindeer shuffled through the door.

"No, problem," the receptionist said.

"RUDOOOOOOOOOOOOLPH!!!"

"He's ready for you," she smiled.

Doctor Kloppen was short and stout with a mop of fire-red hair. He had twinkly green eyes, which Ronaldo thought made him appear friendly, and

Dr.Kloppen

HUGE buck teeth. They were *so* big that
Doctor Kloppen could not close his mouth
properly and kept spitting and dribbling
all the time. (Ronaldo and Rudi had
learned the hard way not to get too close
to him.)

Today, the doctor was wearing a bright
yellow vest and matching shorts, both
stained with dribble.

"Come on in," he spluttered.

"Gross," Rudi whispered. "Where's his
white coat?"

Ronaldo took a seat by the door to
avoid the 'splash zone'. He spotted the jar
of lollipops on the doctor's desk. It was
full and the lid was off.

"Now let's take a look at that hoof, young Rudolph."

Rudi bit his bottom lip, and then held out his arm for Doctor Kloppen to examine.

Yuck! Rudi screwed up his face. Doctor Kloppen was slobbering over his arm.

"And what brings you here, Ronaldo?" the doctor said, moving Rudi's hoof in different directions.

"I'm here as a friend... for moral support."

"Well, I think you deserve a lollipop." Doctor Kloppen chuckled.

"Thanks," Ronaldo said, delving in for a carrot and lemon flavoured one. He looked over his shoulder. *All clear!* He sneaked three more into his pocket. And just in case the doctor forgot about Rudi, he grabbed one for him, too: blackcurrant – Rudi's favourite.

He removed the wrapper from a lollipop and sucked. The lemon flavour fizzled on his tongue.

"This hoof's infected, but nothing a little medicine won't fix," Doctor Kloppen said.

Mrs Gunnersson pulled a tissue from her handbag and mopped her eye.

Rudi stood up and smiled. "All done?"

"Not quite," Doctor Kloppen said. "I just need to give you a teeny weeny injection."

Rudi looked at his mum, his eyes the size of the Beresford summer Ferris wheel.

"It's okay sweetheart, you're nearly finished," she said.

"Bend over, Rudolph," Doctor Kloppen said. "I hear Vixen Pederson's on telly tonight."

"Yes! He's on *The Donna Show*," Ronaldo said, keen to talk about his flying hero.

"He's got a special announcement," Rudi added, relaxing.

Wait a minute! Ronaldo narrowed his eyes. Doctor Kloppen wasn't interested in Vixen, he was purposely distracting Rudi.

The doctor reached into his drawer... and pulled out a needle the size of a rocket!

Ronaldo gasped; sticky lemon trickled down his chin. He turned his back on the others, unwrapped a second lollipop and shoved it in his mouth.

Rudi bent over; his front hooves on his thighs. His eyes darted from left to right, right to left, in alarm.

Doctor Kloppen pulled back Rudi's shorts. They dropped to the floor. Rudi's eyes continued darting from side to side.

Holding the needle up to the light, the doctor gently tapped it with his hoof. He

leant forward.

"Aaaaaaaaaaaaaaah!" Rudi screamed.

The surgery door flew open.

"I'm off to lunch now, Doctor," the receptionist said, waving.

Rudi seized his opportunity... and charged bare-bottomed through the open door... needle and all!

Dribble slavered down Doctor Kloppen's vest. Ronaldo and Mrs Gunnersson rushed to the window. Rudi was bolting from the building like a fox chasing a hare, the needle bouncing up

and down with his every step.

"Ronaldo!" Mrs Gunnersson said in dismay. "Go after him!"

Ronaldo sprinted into the woods. "Rudeeee! Rudeeee!"

He skidded to a halt. The path split four ways. *Which direction did Rudi go?* he pondered. Without snow, there were no hoof prints to follow.

"Aaaaaaaaaaaaaaaaaaaaaah!"

Ronaldo followed the scream. It got louder and louder.

Rudi was up ahead, bouncing up and down like a kangaroo.

"Owww! Something bit me, Ronny," he

shrieked. "I sat down and it bit me. I think it's still on me!"

"Ooooh." Ronaldo winced, imagining the pain Rudi must have felt sitting on the needle.

"Aaaaaah!" Rudi hopped up and down. "It's a giant lizard, Ronny. Help me, help me!"

Ronaldo didn't think the time was right to point out, that even with the current heatwave, there were no lizards in Beresford.

Rudi ran round in circles. Ronaldo chased after him. Round and round and round and round. "Hold still!" Ronaldo called, his head spinning. "I'll get it off you!"

Rudi slowed up. "Quick, Ronny, quick!"

Ronaldo eased the needle from his pal's bottom. "There, all done!" he said, using Doctor Kloppen's favourite line.

Rudi looked over his shoulder. Ronaldo swiftly hid the ginormous needle behind his back.

He was too slow. Rudi had spotted it!

As if in slow motion, Rudi's berry-blue eyes glazed over and his mouth curled into a half smile.

"Aaaah!" He murmured, and passed out.

Chapter Three

Mrs Sorrenson's Scrumptious Carrot Cake

"Thank you so much, Doctor," Mrs Gunnersson said, taking a few steps back to avoid a shower, "and sorry about the mishap earlier." She stroked Rudi's head.

"You're most welcome." Doctor Kloppen frothed at the corners of his mouth. "He should sleep well tonight."

"Say thank you, Rudi."

"Thanks!" Rudi smiled, hugging the lollipop jar to his chest.

Ronaldo shook his head. *Poor Rudi.* He

looked like a team of oxen had trampled him. He wore a sling around his neck to support his hoof, and two huge plasters across his bottom like a giant cross. And Doctor Kloppen had wound a bandage around his head, to protect the enormous bump caused by his fall in the woods. Rudi didn't seem to mind though. He licked a jumbo-sized lollipop, not a care in the world.

The three reindeer left the surgery and strolled down the street.

Mrs Gunnersson hesitated at the

'Carrots 'N' Cakes' bakery. She ogled the mouth-watering gateaux, just like Ronaldo and Rudi had done. "D'you know what?" she said, "I think you two deserve a treat today. Choose a cake – have whatever you want!"

"Yummy!" Rudi said. "Can I have a carrot and chocolate slice?"

Ronaldo stared longingly at the giant carrot cake. "Can I have a piece of that, please?" He licked his lips. His parents only ever bought Mrs Sorrenson's cakes on special occasions.

"Yes, of course," Mrs Gunnersson replied. "I think I'm going to try the carrot and raspberry Pavlova."

The inside of the shop was as enchanting as the outside promised it would be. Pink, blue and white stripes papered the walls. Baby-pink tablecloths with white polka dots completed the decor.

A young doe took the reindeers' order. Her name-badge said she was called Prancy. She showed them to a table by the window and they sat down to wait for their cakes.

Prancy arrived with three enormous wedges.

"Enjoy!" she said, smiling.

Mrs Gunnersson delved into her Pavlova. "This

is divine," she said.

Ronaldo liked to make carrot cake last as long as possible. He closed his eyes and slowly licked frosting from the top.

Unfortunately, the cake was so loaded with cream that a huge dollop dropped from the middle and landed on his vest. *Splat!*

"Come with me," Mrs Gunnersson said. "I'll wash that off before it stains."

Ronaldo reluctantly put down his cake and followed her into the bathroom.

Rudi's chocolate slice melted in the heat. Chocolate oozed over his left hoof.

Buzzzzzzzzz.

A bug! After his sticky cake!

Rudi waved his hoof around

in the air. *Splat!* He missed the bug and slapped his head. "Ouch!"

He was licking chocolate off his hoof, when...

Buzzzzzzzzzzzzz.

He swung round. *Splat!* He hit his head again. "Ouch!"

Buzzzzzzzz. Buzzzzzz. Buzzzzzzzz.

And again... and again... and again.

Rudi swung from left to right, right to left. Chocolate sprayed over the pretty pink tablecloth.

Ronaldo appeared from the bathroom.

"Golly Gosh!" he said, staring at the mess. Rudi's face and hoof were covered in sticky brown goo. His nose was the only chocolate-free zone. And how did he get hoof prints on his bandage?

"Oh, dear!" Mrs Gunnersson sighed.

Buzzzzzzz.

Rudi leant over the table and slammed down his hoof. *BANG!* A blob of chocolate flew up in the air. "Gotcha!" he said, grinning from antler to antler.

Mrs Gunnersson wiped chocolate off her nose. "I think we're going to need more napkins," she said.

Eager to tuck into his cake, Ronaldo sat back down. He curled his tongue and scooped the cream out of the middle.

Mrs Gunnersson pulled up a chair beside him. "Yumm," she groaned. She closed her eyes and disappeared into her own carrot and raspberry Pavlova heaven.

Rudi closed his eyes, too. But not because his cake was delicious. His medicine was making him *extremely* drowsy. He yawned as he chomped away at his delectable chocolate slice, his eyes growing heavier and heavier with every mouthful.

Doink!

Zzzzzzzzzzzzzzzzzzzzzzzz.

Ronaldo and Mrs Gunnersson looked away from their cakes, astonished.

Rudi was face down in the remains of his chocolate slice, his nose now covered in chocolate, too!

Chapter Four

The Mysterious Doe with the Shopping Bags

Ronaldo scampered home. There was an end of term flying exam on Monday morning and he needed to do some revision before Vixen's big interview. He grabbed the last of his lollipops: the blackcurrant one. *Rudi won't miss it*, he thought. Doctor Kloppen had given him more than enough.

A tall reindeer hobbled up the road ahead. *Who's that?* Ronaldo squinted. It looked like a doe, laden with shopping bags.

Ronaldo quickened his pace to help her.

Crack!

A bag split open. Fruit tumbled through the bottom and rolled over the path.

The doe struggled to get down on the floor to pick up her produce.

Ronaldo rushed up. "Let me do it!"

The doe looked up in surprise, her eyes like two giant chocolate buttons. "Oh, thank you so much. It's this hip. I can hardly move at the moment."

She was quite old and wore a lilac blouse with a long blue skirt. Her mousy

hair was twirled into a bun on top of her head. Ronaldo tapped his chin. *Why does she look familiar?*

"My house is close by. Could you carry those in for me, please?" she asked.

"Sure," Ronaldo said, scooping the fruit up in his arms.

The doe smiled. "There might even be a slice of cake in it for you," she said.

"Awesome." Ronaldo grinned. Two slices in one day!

The reindeer fumbled around in her handbag, and mumbled, "Where are my keys?"

Ronaldo's arms quivered. The fruit was heavy. He gritted his teeth: he didn't want it all over the floor again.

"Ah, here they are!"

After following the doe inside, Ronaldo lingered in the hallway, lifted his nose... and sniffed. *How is it possible? This house smells even more delicious than 'Carrots 'N' Cakes' bakery!*

He placed the fruit down on the kitchen table. His eyes widened. Rows and rows of trophies lined the shelves: gold cups with colourful ribbons and sparkly silver statues.

"Wow!" His jaw dropped open. The awards display reached the ceiling.

The doe held out her hoof. "I'm Mrs Sorrenson. And you are?"

"Mrs Sorrenson! Of course!" Ronaldo

said, remembering. He'd seen her photo on the cover of his parents' baking books. "My family loves your cakes."

Mrs Sorrenson chuckled. "Oh, you are kind. But you still haven't told me your name."

"I'm Ronaldo. My house is just down the road. I can't believe I've never seen you before."

"Well, I spend most of my time at home, baking and writing books."

The doe rubbed her hip and winced.

"My grandad's got a hip problem," Ronaldo said. "Doctor Kloppen said it's from too much salsa dancing."

"Oh, I'd love to try salsa," Mrs Sorrenson said, staring into space.

"What happened to *your* hip?"

"I tripped over the rolling-pin. The doctor says I need rest, but there's no time for rest," she wailed. "Six days a week, I have to buy the ingredients from the village, bake the cakes *and* deliver them to 'Carrots 'N' Cakes'."

She limped over to the kitchen cupboard and brought back one of her speciality carrot cakes: just like the one Ronaldo had enjoyed less than half an hour earlier. She cut off a generous portion and handed it to him.

Ronaldo began his ritual of licking the buttery icing off the top. "Scrummy," he drooled.

Mrs Sorrenson nodded her head, satisfied with his reaction.

"Maybe I can help?" he said, scooping cream from the middle of his slice of cake. "I could drop your cakes off at the bakery on my way to Flying School... and do your shopping on the way home." He took another bite. "That way, you can rest your hip," he said, spluttering cake down his shirt.

"That would be wonderful!" Mrs Sorrenson said, tapping her hooves together. "Oh, I'm so grateful. In fact, I think such a good deed deserves another slice of cake, don't you?"

Ronaldo's belly was at bursting-point already. He could hear his parents' voices inside his head: "Don't eat too many sweet things before dinner." *But one more slice wouldn't hurt, would it?* After all, he couldn't offend Mrs Sorrenson.

Ronaldo polished off the second slab of luscious cake. "Delicious," he said, wiping his mouth with the back of his hoof. "Can I wash my hooves before I leave?"

"Of course. The bathroom's just down the hall."

Making sure there wasn't a trace of cream or a single crumb on his fur, Ronaldo washed his face and hooves. His mum, in particular, had eyes like an eagle. He looked at the mirror and smiled. *My parents will never know.*

"I'll see you on Monday morning, Ronaldo."

"Bye!" Ronaldo waved to his new friend and hurried home.

Chapter Five

Wind, Wind and More Wind!

Ronaldo shuffled towards his house. *Grrrrrrr.* His stomach rumbled. *Maybe I shouldn't have eaten that last slice of cake?* His belly had bloated up so much that it looked like he'd swallowed a goat. Fortunately, it was still early. He would have plenty of time to digest the cake before dinner.

He stopped at the doorstep to rub his tummy. Ooooh! It felt like a balloon about to pop.

As he opened the door, the smell of stew hit him in the face like a polar bear's paw. *Yuck!* He covered his mouth, ready to barf.

Phew! Nothing happened.

"Is that you, Ronaldo?" Mum stepped out of the kitchen. "Come with me, come with me," she said with a glint in her eye. "We've got a surprise for you."

Ronaldo visualised the stew and dug his hooves into the carpet. But on second thoughts, he loved surprises. He trotted

to the kitchen.

"Tah dah!" his parents yelled.

The colour drained from Ronaldo's face, and sweat trickled down his fur. His parents were proudly pointing to a... Mrs Sorrenson's carrot cake!

"Mrs Gunnersson said you were so helpful today," Mum explained.

Ronaldo stared at the mountain of cream. His face turned the colour of mushy peas.

"Yum-yum!" He forced his mouth into a smile.

"I'm really looking forward to that

Vixen interview on television," Dad said. He lifted a steaming pot from the stove. Mice and vegetables sloshed around inside and splashed over the sides on to the floor.

Ronaldo heaved. "Oooh!" A wave of sickness flooded through his body

"We're going to eat earlier tonight so we can watch it," Mum said.

"How early?" Ronaldo asked, his voice quivering.

"In about five minutes!"

Five minutes! Ronaldo's face turned as pale as a snowman's bottom. There was no way the stew would fit in his belly. But if he told his parents he felt sick, they would make him go to bed and he would miss Vixen's interview.

His stomach growled loudly.

GRRRRRRRRRRRRRRRRRR.

Then louder still.

GRRRRRRRRRRRRRRRRRRRRRRR.

"Was that your belly?" Dad asked.

"You don't look well." Mum placed her hoof on his forehead. "He's burning up," she said to Dad. "Maybe he's got that flu that's going around."

There are no words to describe the next noise that erupted from Ronaldo's belly. But it was swiftly followed by a mighty belch of which a Tyrannosaurus Rex would have been proud.

BUUUUUUUUUUUUUUUUURP!

The smell of carrot and cinnamon wafted through the kitchen.

Ronaldo's parents sniffed.

"Carrot cake," Dad said.

Mum wrinkled her nose. "That's not just any carrot cake." She breathed in the aroma. "It's a *Mrs Sorrenson's* carrot cake!"

Ronaldo thought Mum had missed her calling in life. She should have been a detective.

"Mrs Gunnersson bought me a piece for helping Rudi," he said.

"Ah! That was nice." Mum smiled.

Ronaldo's belly vibrated like a washing machine as it churned the carrot cake and lollipops, over and over.

BUUUUUUUUUUUURP!

Ronaldo's second burp wasn't as impressive as the first, but a smaller dinosaur would have been very proud of it.

The scent of lemon with a hint of carrot lingered through the kitchen.

His parents sniffed again.

Ronaldo shuffled his hooves. He felt as if he was on trial and waiting to be sentenced.

"Lemon?" Dad said, "With a touch of

carrot."

"Lollipops!" Mum waved her hoof as if she'd cracked an important case.

"Doctor Kloppen gave me a lemon and carrot lollipop." Ronaldo chose his words carefully. His parents didn't need to know about the other lollipops. "He said I was a good friend to Rudi."

"That's true," Mum agreed. "You are a good friend."

Just when Ronaldo thought the investigation was over, his stomach took him by surprise, and he let out another deafening belch.

BUUUUUUUUUUUUUUUUUURP!

Mum narrowed her eyes. "Blackcurrant lollipops!"

She circled around him, her hooves behind her back. "How many lollipops did you eat?"

Ronaldo watched her walk round and round. Round and round. He now felt dizzy *and* sick and sweaty.

"Two," he replied.

"How many?"

"Three." *How did she do it?*

"How many?"

"Four." *Why can't I stop myself?*

"How many?"

"Five!" *It's like she's reading my mind!*

She looked him in the eye and nodded.

"So let me re-cap," Mum said, encircling him again. "You've eaten five lollipops *and* a slice of Mrs Sorrenson's carrot cake *before* dinner?"

Ronaldo's belly rumbled like thunder again... and again. Louder and louder and LOUDER, like a volcano about to erupt.

Unfortunately, the next bout of wind didn't come through Ronaldo's mouth. It blasted through his bottom... and it didn't smell of cinnamon, lemon or blackcurrant!

"Eeeeeeeeew," Mum groaned.

Dad rushed to open a window, only to realise that because of the hot weather, it was already open.

"Sorry," Ronaldo groaned, rubbing his tummy.

"You've been *very* greedy," Mum said, her hooves on her hips. "But I think you've learnt your lesson the hard way."

"Yes," Dad agreed in his most serious voice.

Ronaldo nodded.

"Lie down on the sofa. You can have your dinner later," Mum said.

Ronaldo glimpsed the carrot cake on the table and put his hoof over his mouth.

Ring, ring, ring, ring!

Mum reached for the phone.

Ronaldo pottered into the hallway. *Phew!* He'd been let off the hook.

"Mrs Sorrenson!" Mum squealed. "I'm such a huge fan! We've got all your books."

Mrs Sorrenson! Ronaldo ground to a halt. *What now?!*

"Ronaldo? Yes, he is very helpful," Mum said with pride.

So far, so good. Ronaldo smiled.

"Yes, he loves your carrot cake." She laughed.

"Oh, no!" He groaned.

"Did he?" Mum said.

"*Did he?*" she repeated in a deeper tone.

Ronaldo knew that tone. *I'm done for!*

"He needs to come fifteen minutes earlier on Monday? Okay. Thank you for calling." She put down the phone and sighed.

Ronaldo bit his bottom lip.

"Stop hiding in the hallway and come back in here," Mum called.

How does she know I'm here? He had to admire her policing skills: they were awesome.

"Mrs Sorrenson said you ate not one, but TWO pieces of her speciality carrot cake."

"AND the piece that Rudi's mum bought you?" Dad added. "Even I couldn't manage that!"

Ronaldo looked down at the floor. He wished it would gobble him up.

Mum's voice softened. "She also said you helped her with her shopping *and*

volunteered to deliver her cakes to the
bakery."

"That was kind," Dad said.

Mum kissed her son on his clammy
forehead. "I'm very proud of you," she
said, ruffling his hair.

Ronaldo flunked out on the sofa.
"Aaah!" he moaned. He would never eat
lollipops or carrot cake again! *Not ever.*

Chapter Six

The Vixen Pederson Interview

Ronaldo sprinted like a wolverine through the Forest of Doom. Faster and faster, he ran. An army of lollipops chased after him.

"Seize the prisoner!" ordered Lemontop, their leader.

Ronaldo looked over his shoulder. There were thousands of them! Colossal white sticks with helmets of yellow, orange and purple.

The ground rumbled. Ronaldo staggered. It shook harder. "Yikes!" He fell on his face amongst sharp bracken and broken branches. *Was it an earthquake?*

The lollipops advanced; nearer and nearer. The ground rocked again. Ronaldo looked back. A Tyrannosaurus Rex appeared through the mist. The ground shook with every stamping step it took. It

ploughed through the lollipops, crushing them to smithereens.

Ronaldo tried to stand. "Aargh!" A searing pain shot through his hip.

The dinosaur towered over him. "Would you like a slice of carrot cake?" it growled.

"Noooooooooooo!" Ronaldo screamed.

He opened his eyes and looked around. *Where am I?*

His parents were sitting in armchairs, either side of him.

"Having a bad dream?" Mum asked. "You've woken just in time. The interview's on in a minute."

Ronaldo rolled on to his side so he could see the television.

"Oh, look, there's Vixen!" Dad pointed at the screen.

Ronaldo watched the advert. He'd seen it many times before: It showed Vixen, dressed all in black, roaring along on a snowmobile. He was being chased by wolves. There was a canyon up ahead.

What was he going to do? Vixen stopped and assessed the situation. The wolves gained on him. He revved his engine, steamed through the snow, then soared over the canyon, leaving the wolves far behind.

Vixen looked back over his shoulder, spun his vehicle around and came to a halt. He jumped off and removed his helmet. His thick black quiff fell over one eye.

"Feel your ROARRRR!" he grunted.

Then a voice-over said: "*Reindeer Roar*: The new fragrance by Vixen Pederson."

"So cool," Ronaldo said, spellbound.

"I need to get me some of that," Dad

added.

Gazing at the TV, Ronaldo thought back to the first time he'd met Vixen. His tail fizzled as he remembered the enormous reindeer standing in his kitchen; heard him congratulate him on breaking the endurance record for flying. He still couldn't believe that Vixen Pederson had come to his house that day – just for him.

"Ooh," Mum said. "It's starting."

The presenter, Donna Winkihoff, appeared on the screen, her fair hair styled in a sleek bob. She wore a crisp white shirt beneath a dove-grey pinstriped suit.

"My first guest needs no introduction."

Donna smiled, revealing her dazzling white teeth. "He is Santa's lead reindeer and hero to flying cadets everywhere. Please put your hooves together for Wing Commander Vixen Pederson!"

"Yaaaaaaaaaay!" The studio audience erupted into rapturous applause.

Vixen smiled and waved. He leant forward and kissed Donna on both cheeks.

"So you're here to share some exciting news?" Donna said, flashing a toothy grin.

"That's right," Vixen said in a deep husky voice. "I'm launching a brand-new programme today. It's called The Vixen Pederson Workshop."

"The Vixen Pederson Workshop!" repeated Ronaldo and his parents.

"I think it's important to encourage the youth of today," Vixen continued. "They are the future."

Donna nodded her head. "I couldn't agree with you more."

"I'll be hosting a workshop for two or

three snowflake cadets, every year," Vixen said, "and focusing on team-building activities. At the North Pole, it's essential we work as a team."

"Can any two or three snowflake cadets apply?" Donna asked.

"Yes, but there will be a selection process," Vixen explained. "It's important that cadets work hard and get good grades, so I will be discussing each candidate with Wing Commander Blitsen of The Reindeer Flying Academy."

"How long will the workshop be?" Donna said, crossing her legs. "And what about the cost?"

"The workshop will run for five days and start two weeks before the new term begins. The price is one hundred reindeer roulards, and includes transportation to the location, accommodation, food, and all training."

"That sounds reasonable," said the host, smiling.

"Yes. I want the workshop to be available to as many cadets as possible."

"And where do I sign up?" Donna laughed.

"At The Reindeer Flying Academy. I've been working with Wing Commander Blitsen. She has further information about the workshop and can answer any questions."

Donna moved closer to Vixen. "And finally," she said, "where is the location?"

"It's top secret," Vixen answered, with a smile that would melt most hearts.

"Top secret?!" Donna raised an eyebrow.

"Top secret," Vixen repeated firmly.

The programme ended with the usual pleasantries. But Ronaldo wasn't listening. He was picturing himself flying through the sky with Vixen and Rudi; imagined hanging out with them over hot chocolate in the club-house; laughing and planning their next exciting flight.

"Ronaldo!"

He snapped out of his fantasy.

His parents were staring at him. "Well?" they said.

"It sounds awesome!" Ronaldo sat up. A bit too quickly.

BURP!

"Can I go?"

"Your grades are exceptional," Dad said.

"We think five days with Vixen will really improve your flying skills," Mum added. "Yes, you can go!"

"Yes!" Ronaldo punched the air.

BURP!

"Thanks, Mum and Dad."

"You've earned it!" They said, laughing.

"I better call Rudi." Ronaldo bounced off the sofa. "I hope he didn't sleep through it."

GRRRRRRRRRR.

The sudden movement took his troubled stomach by surprise. A trumpet noise, even louder than Wing Commander Blitsen's horn, blasted through the room.

"Ooooh!" Ronaldo patted his tummy. "On second thoughts, I'll call him later." He flopped back on the sofa.

Dad darted toward the window. This time, he could let in some fresh air!

Chapter Seven

The End of Term Exam

Ronaldo dressed for Flying School. He zipped up his navy blue shorts and buttoned his red short-sleeved shirt. It had two snowflakes on each sleeve to show his rank.

He hurried to Mrs Sorrenson's house. With the exam that morning, he couldn't be late.

He hammered on the door. *Bang, bang, bang!*

Mrs Sorrenson peeked out. She was wearing green patterned pyjamas and had a sprinkling of flour on her nose.

"Good morning, Ronaldo. You're very prompt." She smiled. "Now let me get that cake for you."

She shuffled back holding an enormous box. "Careful, now," she said, passing it over. "It's almost as big as you are."

"Woah!" Ronaldo gripped the box, surprised by how heavy it was. "What's in here, a dead walrus?"

"Bread pudding," Mrs Sorrenson said. "You wouldn't want to fly after a slice of that," she chuckled.

Ronaldo walked as fast as he could with the bulky box. He could only just see over the top.

Voices called *Good Morning* somewhere in the distance. A few

reindeer wandered out of 'Beresford News', flicking through their daily paper.

Ronaldo pushed open the bakery door with his shoulder. He slid the box of cakes on to the counter.

"Good morning, Ronaldo," Prancy said. "Here you go." She gave him two gold coins.

"Thanks, I'll drop them in to Mrs Sorrenson."

He checked the time. It was still quite early. He strolled to The Meeting Point to wait for Rudi: they could walk the rest of the way to school together.

"Morning, Ronny," a couple of cadets called. "D'you see Vixen's interview?"

"I'm signing up for the workshop right now," Vixie said, waving at him as she passed by.

There was a buzz of excitement. The Vixen Pederson Workshop was all anyone could talk about.

Rudi hobbled along the path. He had a

fresh, chocolate-free bandage on his head, and a sling round his neck.

"We'd better sign up for the workshop straight away!" Ronaldo said, giddy with excitement.

"I'm not going," Rudi mumbled.

"What?" Ronaldo laughed. "For a minute there I thought you said you weren't going."

"I did."

"Are you joking?" Ronaldo asked.

"No! I don't wanna go," Rudi said, shrugging his shoulders.

"But yesterday when I phoned, you said

it sounded awesome."

"Changed my mind."

"*Why?*" Ronaldo said, his voice rising with frustration.

"The workshop sounds stupid."

Stupid? Nothing Vixen did was stupid! Maybe the bump to Rudi's head was affecting his judgement? Ronaldo thought to himself.

"Are you feeling okay?" He asked.

"YES!" Rudi snapped. He turned to Ronaldo. "I don't want to go, and I think the whole thing sounds stupid. Got it?!"

He stormed off as quickly as his sore bottom would permit.

Ronaldo stood there, gawping.

Unbeknown to him, three troublesome brothers, Dasher, Comet and Prancer, were lurking in the woods. They'd listened with great interest.

Ronaldo approached The Reindeer Flying Academy. He normally stopped to admire the giant pillars that marked the

magnificent entrance, but a crowd had already gathered around the main notice board. Students were putting their name down for the workshop. Not wanting to miss out, he waited in line and added his name to the list.

"Good morning, Rivaldo!" Wing Commander Blitsen, Ronaldo's senior officer, stood outside the classroom, fanning herself with a clipboard.

Ronaldo gave an enormous sigh. *When will she get my name right?*

The Wing Commander had abandoned her normal flying jacket on such a hot day in favour of a royal blue shirt with six snowflakes on each sleeve. There was a slight frizz to her white hair, although it was still smooth compared to Rudi's mum's.

The desks were separated, ready for the exam. Ronaldo sat by the window hoping to get some fresh air.

Rudi limped to the back of the classroom and sat down. "Ouch!" He winced and jumped up again.

"Let's have you standing up here, Rudolph," Wing Commander Blitsen said, noticing his discomfort.

She slid a cabinet away from the wall.

It was the perfect height for Rudi to write on.

His classmates sniggered. Word had got round about Rudi's recent mishap with the needle.

Ronaldo wanted to yell at them; make them shut up. His friend wasn't in the best mood, but he didn't want anyone laughing at him.

"Settle down now, settle down," Wing Commander Blitsen said in a firm voice. She picked up the examination papers and placed one face down on each desk.

"You have one hour to complete the test. Read the questions *thoroughly*," she said. "Once you have finished, put your paper down on my desk and quietly leave the room."

She looked at the clock. "Your time starts now," she said.

Ronaldo picked up his pencil and turned over the exam paper. He whizzed through page after page. After revising for weeks, he found the test easy.

The navigation section was trickier Hmm. One question, in particular, confused him. He worked out the answer; changed it, then changed it again. Satisfied, he turned the paper over and slammed down his pencil. Finished!

The classroom was silent apart from the scratch of pencils on paper. Ronaldo checked the time: forty-five minutes left.

Wing Commander Blitsen was busy marking papers from another class. Ronaldo remembered her comment on his last report card: *Ronaldo has a tendency to rush and needs to take more care.*

With Vixen's-workshop coming up, it was more important than ever to get a high score. Ronaldo grabbed his pencil. He would double-check and triple-check every answer.

Cadets were leaving the classroom. Ronaldo took no notice. He spotted a couple of mistakes. He rubbed them out and changed his answers.

Grateful he had remembered Wing Commander Blitsen's advice, he placed his paper on her desk and crept outside.

Prancer and Comet were by the door. Ronaldo presumed they were waiting for their brother, Dasher. The trio stuck together like toffee.

They're troublemakers! I'll wait by the trees for Rudi, Ronaldo thought to himself.

His friend was last to leave the classroom.

"I'm really, really looking forward to Vixen's workshop," Dasher said in a loud voice. He blocked Rudi's way.

"Me too!" Prancer said.

"And me," Comet said, giggling.

"Are you looking forward to it, Rudolph?" Dasher sneered.

Rudi looked at Dasher, his bottom lip trembling.

"Oh, I forgot," Dasher said. "*You're* not going!" he said with a smirk.

"TREAT your classmates with kindness and respect, flying cadets!"

The brothers jumped in surprise. Wing Commander Blitsen stood behind them, her hooves on her hips and her nostrils flaring. She stooped forward, "Or there will be no Vixen Pederson Workshop for you three!"

The Commander marched off.

Rudi tottered away.

Ronaldo called after him. "Rudi, wait for me!"

Rudi turned round, "Go away, Ronny!" he barked. "Just leave me alone!"

Ronaldo watched, opened-mouthed, as his pal disappeared through the main exit and into the woods.

Chapter Eight

Grumpy Ronny

Ronaldo stomped home. He was furious with Rudi. *How dare he call Vixen's workshop stupid? And who did he think he was, yelling at me?* He opened the front door and slammed it shut.

"Sorry," he called out.

Mum popped her head out of the kitchen. She noticed the scowl on her son's face. "I've just made some fresh carrotade. Would you like some?"

"Yes, please."

Ronaldo plonked himself down.

Mum brought a yellow beaker

with a red and white striped straw to the kitchen table. "Didn't the exam go well?" she asked.

"The exam was fine. It's stupid Rudi!" Ronaldo growled.

"Rudi?" Mum said with surprise.

"He said Vixen's workshop is stupid, and that he doesn't want to go."

"Ah," Mum said as if she understood. "I heard today that the Gingerbread Factory is closing down."

"Aw!" Ronaldo moaned. "I love their gingerbread."

He sucked through the straw. The ice-cold juice felt good on his dry throat.

Then he realised what his mum meant. "Rudi's dad works there!"

"Exactly! I bumped into him on my rounds this morning. He was awfully upset. Said he planned to give Rudi the best birthday party ever, but that he can't afford the workshop as well... not until he finds another job."

Ronaldo put his hoof under his chin. "I feel bad now, going on about it like I did."

Mum looked thoughtful. "Maybe Rudi can go next year?" she said. "Why don't you focus more on his birthday party? His dad said they've booked some special magician: Mervin the Moose?"

"*Monty*!" Ronaldo corrected. "Monty the Moose."

"Is he the one on the telly?"

"Yeah. He's not a real moose. He wears a mask... but he's super cool."

Thump, thump, thump! Thump, thump,

thump! Someone was at the door.

Ronaldo sprang up to answer it. "It's Rudi! That's our secret knock."

Rudi stood on the doorstep. He looked sadder than a fawn with no Christmas presents.

"I'm sorry, Ronny."

"It's okay." Ronaldo smiled. "D'you wanna practice card tricks?"

"Yes!" Rudi flashed a smile. "My dad made carrot babas." He held up a bag.

Ronaldo never wanted to lay eyes on carrot cake ever again. But he had nothing against babas!

Chapter Nine

The Mrs Sorrenson Cake Incident

"Morning," Ronaldo said cheerfully.

"There are two cakes for the bakery today," Mrs Sorrenson said. She put her hoof over her mouth and yawned. "Please take care. I've been up since five baking them."

"Don't worry." Ronaldo peeked over the top of the boxes. "They're in safe hooves."

He walked with a spring in his step towards Beresford village. Rudi's party was getting closer. He couldn't wait to see

Monty the Moose!

"Whatcha got there, Rotten Ronny?"

"Oh, no!" Ronaldo muttered under his breath. If only he'd taken a different path.

Dasher, Comet and Prancer were slouching against the trees; arms folded across their chests. Dasher strutted towards him. "What's in the boxes?" he said, glaring at Ronaldo. The white patch around his left eye stood out against his chestnut fur.

"None of your business!" said a stifled voice.

Dasher moved closer. He placed his

hooves around the top box.

"Leave it alone," Ronaldo said, taking a firmer grip.

Dasher tugged at the box.

"Go on Dash!" Comet urged his brother. "Find out what's inside."

Dasher yanked harder.

Ronaldo pulled back.

The two fawns wrestled over the box.

"Daaa-sher! Daaa-sher!" Prancer and Comet cheered.

"Let go!" Ronaldo yelped.

Dasher grinned. "Okay." He waved his hooves in the air.

"Yikes!" Ronaldo lost balance. He

stumbled backwards, struggling to keep hold of the two boxes. He slipped and slithered on a patch of mud in his desperate attempt to remain standing.

"Aaaaaargh!" Ronaldo lost control.

Thump!

He landed flat on his back. The cake box flew out of his arms.

"Noooooooooo!" he yowled.

Ronaldo watched helplessly as the box soared higher and higher above him, and then crashed into a tree.

Wallop!

It dropped on to the ground.

Splat!

Ronaldo sat up, clutching the second box like a mother wolf protecting her cub.

Dasher shrugged his shoulders. "You told me to let go."

Comet and Prancer cackled and squealed in delight. They sounded as if they'd been sucking on helium balloons.

Ronaldo scowled. Mrs Sorrenson had

been up all morning baking that cake. His face, already flushed from the heat, grew redder and redder and REDDER! His heart thumped like a ticking bomb. He was ready to explode!

"Ha-ha-ha!" The brothers cavorted around in stitches of laughter.

Ronaldo opened the second box, and carefully lifted a super-creamy carrot cake from inside. He scrambled up to stand on his back hooves and drew the cake on to his shoulder, like a shot-putter in the Olympic Games. With all of his might, he hurled the cake at Dasher's face.

Bullseye!

Ronaldo and Dasher stared at each other in shock.

Comet and Prancer laughed hysterically at their brother's cake-splattered face.

"SHUUUDUP!" Dasher screamed.

Ronaldo's head swam. *Why did I throw the cake?*

"Ooh, it tastes good," Comet said, licking his brother's cheek.

"I want some too," Prancer said, swiping cake from Dasher's face.

"GET OFF!!!!!!!!!!!!" Dasher thundered. He stomped off with his sniggering brothers in pursuit.

Ronaldo slumped down on a tree stump. *He* had destroyed one of Mrs Sorrenson's cakes. What was he going to do now?

If he told Mrs Sorrenson that Dasher

and his brothers had ambushed him, she might have been sympathetic. But, if he told her he had thrown the second cake, she would think he was irresponsible. She wouldn't trust him anymore. And what about her money – her ten roulades for each cake?

"Nooooo!" Ronaldo put his head in his hooves.

He had an idea! *What if I tell Prancy that Mrs Sorrenson isn't feeling well and hasn't baked any cakes today? I can say not to telephone her, as she needs rest. Then I can take twenty roulards from my money box and give it to Mrs Sorrenson.*

But what about Rudi's birthday present? He pouted. *Something less expensive would have to do.*

Satisfied the plan would work, Ronaldo sprinted to the bakery to inform Prancy that Mrs Sorrenson was sick. Tomorrow, he would take a different route into the village. And he would stay out of trouble!

Chapter Ten

Mr Gunnersson's Babas

BURP! "I'm stuffed," Rudi said, rubbing his belly.

BURP! "Me too," Ronaldo said.

The two fawns strolled back from Lake St Nicholas. They'd had a picnic to celebrate passing their end of term exam: carrot babas, carrot and grass babas, and carrot and cranberry babas.

And Ronaldo had another reason to feast: his exam result was so good that he had been one of the first selected for The Vixen Pederson Workshop.

Rudi had been babbling non-stop about

his magic hero, Monty the Moose.

"D'you think he'll do that trick with the lemmings at my party?" he asked.

"I hope so: I crack-up every time he does it," Ronaldo chuckled.

"It's two weeks today until my birthday. And three until Vixen's workshop," Rudi said.

"I wish you were coming."

"Me too."

"I think I'll pop by Mrs Sorrenson's," Ronaldo said, as they arrived at The Meeting Point. "She might like some company."

"Okay, see ya tomorrow," Rudi said, waving. "It's gonna be a big day!"

"Good luck," Ronaldo called. His friend had a last minute medical in the morning. The doctor would decide if he was fit to fly.

Ronaldo arrived at the baker's house and hammered on the front door.

"Yes!!!" Mrs Sorrenson appeared, her face the colour of a red hot chilli pepper. Her hair was sprinkled with so much flour that Ronaldo wondered if any had actually made it into her cakes.

"Oh," Ronaldo said, taking a step back. "D'you want me to come back tomorrow?"

"No. Please come on in," she said with a small smile. "I'm having rather a bad day."

"What's wrong?" Ronaldo asked, following her inside.

Woah! Mrs Sorrenson's cosy kitchen looked as if a herd of moose had stampeded through it. A mountain of flour and butter hid the counter tops. The bin exploding with discarded cakes.

"It's me! I'm what's wrong! All these awards," she said, pointing to her display, "and all these baking books, but for the life of me, I cannot bake a baba!"

"Rudi's dad bakes fantastic babas," Ronaldo said, rummaging around his picnic hamper. "I think I've got one left."

He offered the sticky cake to Mrs Sorrenson; licked syrup from his hoof.

The doe sniffed it, closed her eyes, and took a large bite.

"Hmmmmmmmmmm," she moaned.

"It's beautifully light." She delved in a second time. "And so moist. It's the best I've ever tasted!"

"Rudi's dad used to work at The Ginger Bread Factory," Ronaldo explained. "But he lost his job when it closed down."

Mrs Sorrenson raised an eyebrow. "Did he now?" she said, polishing off the remains of the baba. Her face lit up like a twinkling star.

She's really enjoying that baba! Ronaldo thought.

The doe took a jug of carrotade from the fridge. "What's your grandad up to nowadays?" she said, pouring some of the bright orange juice into two glasses.

"Skydiving!"

"*Skydiving!*" Mrs Sorrenson looked up. Carrotade ran over the counter top.

"My nan's doing it, too. They're gonna miss Rudi's party, which is a shame."

"I do love hearing about your family's adventures," Mrs Sorrenson said. She

sat down. "It really makes me think. I've spent my entire life working, and there are so many other things I'd like to do."

"Like what?"

"Well, I'm not sure I'd be a very good skydiver," she said, "but I would certainly love to try a salsa class. Or ballroom dancing." She gazed into the distance for a moment. Then she leant over and topped up Ronaldo's juice. "Are you excited about the Reindeer Flyover tomorrow?" she asked.

"Yes!" Ronaldo grinned from antler to

antler. "I'm lead reindeer," he said, puffing out his chest.

He looked at the time. "I'd better go! I need to go through the flight plan one more time... and make sure my uniform's pressed and ready."

After guzzling his juice, Ronaldo climbed down from the table. "Thanks for the drink," he said.

"Don't forget your picnic hamper," Mrs Sorrenson said, laughing.

"Oh, yeah," Ronaldo chuckled.

"See you in the morning!" The doe smiled.

"Byeeeeee!" Ronaldo rushed out of the door.

Chapter Eleven

FrizzNo Fever!

Ronaldo peered out through his bedroom window. A cloudless blue sky, not a breath of wind: perfect conditions for flying!

The Reindeer Flyover was an ancient tradition of The Reindeer Flying Academy

to mark the end of term. It dated back centuries: flying cadets flew over the district, to the delight of cheering crowds below. Ronaldo remembered watching the Reindeer Flyover when he was small, woozy with excitement, and dreaming that one day he would be up there, too.

After carefully styling his hair and polishing his antlers until they gleamed, he gave a satisfied nod to his reflection. He then folded his flying jacket, and put it in his backpack, together with his goggles and leggings.

He jogged to Mrs Sorrenson's house.

"Can you go as quickly as possible on your deliveries?" Mrs Sorrenson asked. "The weather's so hot and sticky today that I'm worried the icing will melt."

"Sure," Ronaldo said.

"Good luck," she said, "I'll be waving at you."

Ronaldo took a different path as planned. He hurried so that the icing wouldn't melt but also because he wanted to arrive early at Flying School. It was an exciting day. He couldn't wait to soak up the atmosphere.

He heard a commotion in the distance. Loud voices... and lots of them. He stopped and listened. The village was usually quiet at this time of the morning, but it sounded as if there was a Northern Lights Stadium crowd there right now! He plodded on. The noises got louder and louder.

"Be careful with those antlers, you nearly poked my eye out!" an angry doe yelled.

"Stop pushing in!" bawled another.

What's going on? Ronaldo lowered the cake box. *Goodness!* More reindeer scurrying around than at the Annual Snowman Festival!

"Woah!" A crazy reindeer barged past Ronaldo, almost knocking the box out of his hooves. Ronaldo swiveled round.

"Dad, is that you?"

Ronaldo watched open-mouthed as his dad bulldozed his way through a rabble outside Snowflakes Department Store: an unruly rabble that trailed from the front of the blue and white building right back through the village.

The crowd couldn't be for the Reindeer Flyover. It wasn't customary to gather in the village. *So why is everyone here?*

"Excuse me," Ronaldo said. "Can I get by?"

He weaved in and out of the hordes of reindeer, hugging the cake box tightly to his chest.

"Phew!" He slipped through the bakery door. "It's pandemonium out there!" he said to Prancy. "What's going on?"

"*FrizzNo* fever."

"*FrizzNo* what?" Ronaldo said, confused.

"*FrizzNo* is a new hair product being released today. Everyone's gone mad for it! It's supposed to combat frizz."

"All those reindeer are here to buy a hair product?"

"Yeah. I'm hoping I can take my break early today." Prancy ran her hooves over her fuzzy locks. "I'm worried the store's gonna sell out."

Ronaldo peered through the door. "I'm scared to go back out there!"

Prancy opened the cake box. Ronaldo held his breath. *What if the icing had melted?*

"Ooh. That looks delicious," she said.

Ronaldo sighed with relief as Prancy carefully placed the cake in the window.

He looked through the front door again. There were masses of reindeer, even more than before.

"Shouldn't you be off to school?" Prancy said.

Ronaldo couldn't be late; it was the most important day of the year.

He opened the door, lowered his head, and charged his way through the frizz-fest like an angry hippo.

Chapter Twelve

The Reindeer Flyover

Rudi rushed up to Ronaldo, waving both his arms. "I'm fit to fly!!!"

"Yes!" Ronaldo thumped the air.

"Doctor Kloppen took my bandage off, too."

"Did he?" Ronaldo looked closer. The

fur where the bandage had been was paler than it was on the rest of Rudi's face. From a distance, he looked like he was still wearing it.

Rudi held up an elastic support. "He says I've got to wear this over my hoof."

Out of the corner of his eye, Ronaldo spotted Dasher. He waved at Ronaldo, a menacing smile upon his face. Comet and Prancer whispered in their brother's ear. The trio sniggered. *Were they plotting something?*

Ronaldo shuddered. *What if Dasher wants revenge for the cake incident? Would he sabotage the Reindeer Flyover? I am lead reindeer. Wing Commander*

Blitsen will hold me responsible if anything goes wrong!

"Line up!!!" Wing Commander Blitsen ordered.

Ronaldo feared the worst. His bottom lip quivered.

The Wing Commander clapped her hooves together with excitement. "Today's the day!"

Standing by a large map which showed the routes for each year, she pointed to it with her hoof. "Just to re-cap: fly north west over the village... When you approach Heigh Ho, perform a U-turn."

Ronaldo stared into space, imagining a reindeer pile-up. He pictured his classmates splattered over Heigh Ho Hill and Wing Commander Blitsen in floods of tears.

"It's Ronaldo's fault," everyone would say. "Vixie should have been lead reindeer!"

The Commander turned to her

students. "Keep at the lower altitude like we practiced. We want everyone to get a good look at you." She smiled. "And follow Ronaldo's lead."

Rudi nudged Ronaldo with his elbow. "She got your name right, for once."

"What?" Ronaldo said. He'd been busy envisioning, 'Reindeer Flyover Disaster' headlines in *The Weekly Flyer*, instead of paying attention.

The Officer walked slowly down the line of flying cadets. "Today is all about teamwork," she said. "And those of you hoping to be on The Vixen Pederson

Workshop," she hovered in front of Dasher, "be sure to give your best performance." She looked Dasher right in the eye.

Ronaldo let out a tremendous sigh of relief. Dasher wouldn't risk missing Vixen's workshop, and Comet and Prancer wouldn't do anything sinister without their brother.

The Wing Commander checked her watch. "Time to gear up!"

Ronaldo and Rudi changed into their flying jackets and leggings.

Wing Commander Blitsen handed out red hats with two snowflakes embroidered on each side. "These are collector's items," she said, "so look after them."

With his hat fastened under his chin, Ronaldo pushed his goggles up on to his forehead and took his spot on the runway.

The other nineteen cadets followed suit.

"Three minutes to go," Wing

Commander Blitsen said, inspecting her troop. "Prepare your goggles."

She placed a hoof on Ronaldo's shoulder. "You can do this!" she whispered into his ear.

Confidence raced through Ronaldo's body. *Yes, I can!*

A hush settled over The Reindeer Flying Academy as cadets prepared for take-off, each class on a different runway.

Ronaldo panted. His jacket and hat were making him sweat like a bear in a sauna.

Bong, Bong, Bong....... the village clock chimed ten times in the distance.

"This is it!" the Wing Commander barked. She raised her horn and blew.

TOOT-TOOT-TOOT-TOOOO!!!

As a fanfare of horns rang out over the Academy, Ronaldo galloped along the runway.

"Faster," he shouted to his teammates, who were following behind.

Sensing his speed was right, Ronaldo leapt into the sky. "Take-off!" he screamed. Cool mountain air hit him in the face. It was blissful after the stuffiness on the ground.

Ronaldo checked his compass and flew in a north-westerly direction.

"Straighten up!" he bellowed.

"Straighten, up!" Vixie repeated. Ronaldo's command echoed along the line.

As far as the eye could see, Reindeer stood outside their homes, waving up at the sky. Ronaldo spotted his mum and dad and Mrs Sorrenson. He felt his mouth curl into a huge smile.

Woosh! The herd swooped like birds over Lake St Nicholas. Reindeer in sun hats and colourful bathing costumes jumped up and down below.

A faint cheer rang out. Ronaldo's tail tingled with pride.

"Stay focused," he yelled over his shoulder.

Glancing to his right, Ronaldo spotted the first-form cadets in their one-snowflake jackets. *Perfect positioning,* he thought to himself. *Exactly as they'd rehearsed!*

The sky-high red and white clock tower drew nearer.

"Here we go!" Ronaldo hollered.

The village was jam-packed. A queue from Snowflakes Department Store wound through it like a slithering snake.

"Look at all those reindeer," Vixie squealed, from behind.

Unbelievable! Ronaldo thought to himself.

The first-year cadets flew beneath him. *Not bad!* Two of them were a little far apart, but in general, they were doing a fine job.

A class of three snowflake cadets whooshed over Ronaldo's head.

"Hi, Ronneeeeee," shouted his cousin, Cupid.

The fourth and fifth-form cadets flew above them.

Ronaldo peered down at the fuzzy-haired mob swarming in the village. He watched them bounce up and down and wave their hooves in the air.

"Nuttier than pecan pie," he said, chuckling to himself.

Heigh Ho loomed in the distance. Once a popular spot for sledging, it had recently been transformed into a family picnic area. Ronaldo sailed past the luscious green hill, dotted with red and white checked blankets and wicker baskets.

"Woohooo!" Sun hats scattered into the air.

Ronaldo wrinkled his forehead. It was time for the U-turn; a difficult manoeuvre that his class had struggled with in training.

"Prepare for U-turn!" he commanded.

Checking his compass, he swished his tail to the side and turned... and turned.

He approached the end of the troop. Rudi was keeping perfect pace at the back.

"You're doing great!" he called over his shoulder. (Wing Commander Blitsen had told him it was important to encourage his squad.)

He glanced back. Rudi had swung around and was now in line with the group behind him.

"Perfect!" he hollered. "Well done!"

With the hard part over and the homeward stretch in sight, Ronaldo tried to savour the rest of the flight. After all, it was his last time as a two-snowflake cadet.

He proudly led his team-mates back over the village. The summer Ferris wheel whizzed round and round below them. The passengers on board cheered and waved.

"Lower altitude," Ronaldo ordered. The runway was up ahead!

"Lower altitude," Vixie repeated.

Wing Commander Blitsen stood near

the top of the runway, one hoof shielding her eyes from the sun.

"Prepare for landing!" Ronaldo lowered his hind legs. Everyone followed suit.

"Slow right down and space out!" he barked.

Ronaldo's back legs touched down. He leant forward a little and dropped his front hooves. After drifting to a halt, he scrambled to the side of the airstrip to make room for Vixie.

He watched in amazement as one by one, his classmates expertly dropped from the sky. *Wow!* Even Dasher, Comet and Prancer had done themselves proud.

His colleagues joined him by the side of the runway. Rudi was last to land. Ronaldo and the rest of the class cheered him on, as he touched down.

"Yayyyyyyyyyyyyy!!!!" The whole class unfastened their hats and hurled them into the air.

"Fantastic! You were all fantastic," Wing Commander Blitsen bawled.

"That was brilliant!" Rudi said, scurrying around on the grass, searching for his hat. "The village looked bonkers. Did you see all those reindeer?"

The class gathered around Wing Commander Blitsen. "Congratulations, flying cadets. I'm so proud of you!" She dabbed her eyes with a tissue. "I'll see you back here next term... as *three*-snowflake cadets!"

"Yippeeee!" they whooped with joy.

"There are treats for you outside the main hut!" she said, beaming.

The hut was bursting with excitement. Flying cadets from all over the academy high-fived each other in celebration. The atmosphere was electric!

Rows and rows of tables lined the grass. They were piled high with carrot and apple pizza and carrot and lemming quiche. Cupcake towers rose from the centre of each table. Carrot and raisin baguettes were clustered around them.

"They've got your favourite, Ronny," Rudi said, grabbing a giant slab of Mrs Sorrenson's carrot cake."

Ronaldo thought back to the last time he had eaten carrot cake. He shuddered.

"I think I'll have pizza today," he said.

Chapter Thirteen

Mrs Sorrenson's Apprentice

One afternoon, when Rudi had a doctor's appointment to check on his hoof, Ronaldo decided to visit Mrs Sorrenson. He enjoyed chatting with the old doe, and he'd be sure to get a slice of cake.

As he strolled down the path, he spotted Rudi's dad coming the opposite way. He was bouncing along and whistling a merry tune.

"Hi, Mr Gunnersson," Ronaldo said.

"Good afternoon." Mr Gunnersson raised his straw trilby hat.

Ronaldo stared at his hair. *It had turned blue!*

"Can't stop, got something important to do." Mr Gunnersson whooshed past.

"Okay, bye," Ronaldo said, waving.

Mrs Sorrenson greeted Ronaldo with a wide smile and sparkling eyes. "Come on in, I'm having a little celebration," she said.

"It's not your birthday is it?" Ronaldo hoped it wasn't. He didn't have enough money for a present for Mrs Sorrenson *and* Rudi.

She took a fresh flowery tablecloth from the cupboard and laid it on the kitchen table.

"Firstly, my hip is better, thanks to you." She smiled, and placed a mountain of carrot Bakewell slices in the middle of the table. "And secondly, I'm retiring!"

"What?" Ronaldo said in a high-pitched voice. *How will I survive without Mrs Sorrenson's cakes?*

"Don't worry," she said patting his hoof. "I've employed an apprentice."

"What's an apprentice?"

"It's someone you train to do your job." She poured two glasses of carrotade. "I've found the perfect candidate."

Ronaldo remembered seeing Mr Gunnersson. "Is it Rudi's dad?!"

"Yes! I've hired him to bake my cakes under the *Mrs Sorrenson* name."

The doe's eyes glistened as she spoke. "I'm going to take that salsa class... and I have an invitation to Rudi's party tomorrow." Her face shone brighter than Donna Winkihoff's teeth.

She looks ten years younger, Ronaldo thought to himself.

Mrs Sorrenson topped up his juice. "On a serious note, I have something to ask you."

Oh, no! Ronaldo wriggled in his seat. She had the same expression his mum had whenever he was in trouble.

"Ronaldo, why did you tell Prancy that I was sick a few weeks ago? And what happened to those two cakes you didn't deliver to her?"

Ronaldo looked down at his hooves. *What should I tell her?* Grandad always said to take responsibility for his actions. He had done a good job recently, so maybe Mrs Sorrenson wouldn't be too hard on him. He took a deep breath and told her what had happened that day.

Mrs Sorrenson listened patiently. She picked up her glass and took a big gulp of juice.

"I was so angry," Ronaldo said, remembering back, "I took the cake and threw it at him."

The baker choked on her juice, her eyes the size of carrot and lemon meringue pies.

She coughed and spluttered. Carrotade spurted from her mouth. She put her hand to her chest, gasped for breath, and watched cross-eyed as juice erupted from her nose.

"Shall I get Doctor Kloppen?" Ronaldo said, alarmed at the orange explosion.

Mrs Sorrenson waved her hoof. Her

shoulders shook up and down. She threw her head back... and roared with laughter.

"Oh, Ronaldo," she said, tears running down her cheeks, "a bully deserves a cake in the face." She put her hoof to the side of her mouth. "But don't tell your parents I said that."

Ronaldo chuckled. He was relieved she wasn't upset with him.

"But where did you get the money to pay me?"

"It was my pocket money."

"Oh, no," she said, reaching for her purse. "I can't take your money."

Ronaldo shook his head firmly. "I threw the cake. It was my fault."

"But the first cake wasn't. Let's split it fifty-fifty." She placed ten roulards into his hoof.

"Okay," Ronaldo said. He'd have a bit more money to spend on Rudi's present. "It's a deal. Thank you!"

Mrs Sorrenson leaned forward and

gently covered his hoof with her own. "Have Dasher and his brothers done anything like that to you before?"

"Yeah. They're mean to everyone... but they do seem to pick on me the most."

"Promise me that if anything like that happens again, you'll tell your parents... or come to me."

Ronaldo nodded. "Thanks," he said.

"Good job it wasn't my bread pudding," Mrs Sorrenson said with a grin. "You'd have knocked him out!"

"Ha-ha-ha!" They laughed and laughed.

Mrs Sorrenson stared at her purse on the table. "Oh, no!" She threw her hooves to her face. "How silly am I? I haven't paid you!"

"You just did," Ronaldo said with a confused expression.

The doe smiled: Ronaldo's face resembled a blank sheet of paper. "No! For delivering my cakes! You didn't think I was expecting you to do it for nothing?"

She sighed softly. "What a gem, you are, Ronaldo!" she said.

She counted out forty-five roulards and slid the gold coins along the tablecloth towards him. "Here are three roulards for each day," she said. "And," she delved into her purse again, "as you expected nothing in return and helped me out of the goodness of your heart... I'm going to double that!"

"*Double it?*" Ronaldo stared at the pile of shiny coins. There were ninety in total. So with the ten, she'd already given him, he had one hundred reindeer roulards!

"I have to go," he said, and scooped the money into his hooves. He jumped up, leaving a slice of half-eaten cake on his plate.

Mrs Sorrenson laughed. "Don't go spending it all at once," she said.

"I'm afraid I'm going to!" Ronaldo bolted from the house. "Thank you," he called, over his shoulder.

Now he could give Rudi the best birthday present, ever!

Chapter Fourteen

An Unexpected Encounter

Floodlights from The Reindeer Flying Academy illuminated the woods. Wing Commander Blitsen was hosting a special night-flying workshop for fifth-formers.

"Where's Wing Commander Blitsen?" Ronaldo called to a group of cadets, who were already heading out.

"In her office," they called back.

Ronaldo sprinted through the aerodrome towards the officers' building. He raced down the corridor and slid to a stop outside the Commander's office. He smoothed his hair off to one side and knocked on the door.

"Come in!" her deep voice boomed.

Ronaldo barged in and dropped the coins in a heap on her desk.

Wing Commander Blitsen stared at them in surprise.

"It's... for... Rudi," Ronaldo puffed and panted. "For Vixen's... workshop." He rubbed at the side of his ribs. He'd given himself a stitch.

"Oh, Rivaldo. I am sorry. The workshop's already full."

"*What?*" Ronaldo couldn't believe it. "Full?"

"I'm afraid so. Mr Gunnersson came by

earlier. I told him the same thing."

"But Rudi got eighty percent in his exam," he said, his voice shaking. This couldn't be right!

"Why don't you sit down for a moment?" the Wing Commander said. "You look like you've flown to the North Pole and back."

Ronaldo slumped down, devastated. The workshop wouldn't be half as much fun without Rudi.

"Where did you get all this money?"

Ronaldo explained how Mrs Sorrenson had rewarded him. He looked up at his commanding officer. He blinked. Maybe it was the light, but her hair seemed to have turned blue.

"It's such a shame. As you say, Rudi did exceptionally well in his exam," She sighed. "Maybe he can go on next year's workshop."

Ronaldo managed a weak smile. "Yeah," he said.

With his head hung low, he plodded along the corridor. He almost wished Mrs Sorrenson hadn't given him the money. Then he wouldn't have built his hopes up.

Smack!

As he turned the corner, Ronaldo bounced off what felt like a brick wall. He staggered, waving his arms like a windmill, and landed on his backside.

"Are you alright, Ronny?"

A handsome reindeer with antlers like those of a moose, and eyes the colour of liquorice fudge, looked down on him. An immaculate black quiff hung low on his forehead.

"Vixen Pederson!" Ronaldo's face broke into a huge smile. His spirits lifted.

The superstar reindeer reached out a hoof to help Ronaldo up.

Ronaldo caught a whiff of scent: lemon and lavender, with a hint of peppermint. *Reindeer Roar!* When he grew up, he wanted to smell just like that!

"I'm really looking forward to your workshop," he said, brushing himself down.

Vixen's face glowed with enthusiasm. "I've got so many fantastic things planned," he said. "I'm here to finalise a few details with Blitsy."

"Blitsy?"

"Wing Commander Blitsen to you," Vixen laughed.

"How long are you here for?" Ronaldo asked.

"A few days. Why?"

Ronaldo grinned and crossed his arms over his chest. He had a brainwave!

"Would you like to come to a party?"

Chapter Fifteen

Rudi's Near-Disastrous Birthday Party!

Ronaldo taped a card to Rudi's present. He had bought his friend a pair of luminous lime *Super* FLY-X goggles. Top of the range. He had also treated himself to a pair with the money Mrs Sorrenson had given him. *I'll be wearing my new goggles in one week's time, at The Vixen Pederson Workshop!* He shivered with delight.

He had placed Rudi's gift inside a box, then inside another box, and another one. And then wrapped the boxes in ten

sheets of wrapping paper, all of different designs. He giggled. *Rudi's going to have fun opening my present.*

"Are you ready?" Dad called up the stairs.

"Coming!" Ronaldo called back.

Butterflies somersaulted in his tummy. He was beside himself with excitement about seeing Monty the Moose. Plus, he had a surprise up his sleeve which he hadn't even told his parents about. Vixen Pederson was coming to the party!

Dad was waiting in the hallway. Ronaldo

stopped on the stairs, his eyes bulging.

Dad's hair, although smartly combed, looked bright blue. *Another one! Was there something in the water?* Ronaldo had better be careful: *he* didn't want to look like a blueberry bonbon.

"We've forgotten to buy Rudi a present," Mum said, rushing down the stairs.

"All taken care of," Ronaldo said, holding up the giant box.

"Oh, that's a relief." Mum reached for her coat. "Put your jacket on, Ronaldo. It's a lot cooler today."

"What did you get for Rudi?" Dad asked.

"It's a surprise," Ronaldo replied.

"Is it a puzzle?"

Ronaldo shook his head.

"Is it colouring pencils?"

Mum rolled her eyes.

Dad continued to guess all the way to Rudi's house. He didn't guess right.

Colourful balloons lined the path to the party.

"Oh, doesn't it look festive?" Mum said, as they trotted towards the turquoise and yellow cottage.

Unfortunately, Mrs Gunnersson, who was also sporting bluish hair, didn't look festive at all. She was sitting on a wall outside her house with her head in her hooves. Mrs Sorrenson was patting her on the shoulder.

"What's wrong?" Dad asked.

"It's Monty the Moose!"

"What about him?" Ronaldo said in a panicked voice.

"He's not coming," she whimpered. "He's got the fluuuuuuuuuu."

"*Monty the Moose isn't coming?*" Ronaldo screeched.

"Sshhhh!" Mrs Gunnersson looked over her shoulder. "We haven't told Rudi yet."

"What are you going to do?" Ronaldo's mum whispered.

"I don't know. We bought him *The Monty Magic Kit*," Mrs Gunnersson said, sniffing. "It's got a very nice cape."

"Maybe Rudi will be so delighted that he'll forget about Monty," Mrs Sorrenson said, trying to cheer her up.

"D'you really think so?"

Not a chance, Ronaldo thought. Rudi had been harping on about Monty for weeks.

Rudi appeared on the doorstep, a pink party hat with purple swirls perched on his head.

"Muuu-m," Rudi called, "when's Monty coming?"

"Any minute now," she chirped. "I'll call you the second he arrives."

Mrs Gunnersson waited until he had gone back inside, then broke down again. "Oh, I can't bear it. He's gonna be heartbroken!"

Ronaldo cocked his head to one side. *Should I tell her about Vixen coming? It might soften the blow.*

Someone whistled nearby. Ronaldo swiveled round.

"Do you hear that?" he said.

"I do," Dad replied. "Sounds familiar..."

Ronaldo pricked his ears. "It's the theme tune to *The Monty the Moose Magic Show.*"

The five reindeer craned their necks to look down the path.

Walking towards them, like a vision from Heaven, was a tall moose carrying a large case. A long red cape hung from his shoulders, and he wore yellow and red checked dungarees with a spotted bow tie.

The tie was whizzing round and round.

"Good afternoon." He raised his black silk top hat. "I'm Monty the Moose!"

Everyone shouted at once.

"Rudeeeeeeeeeeeeeeeeeeeeeeeeeeeee!!!"

Chapter Sixteen

Monty the Moose?

"Anyone in the mood for magic?" Monty the Moose called out.

"Yes!!!" The fawns screamed.

"I said, anyone in the mood for MAGIC?!" Monty cupped his ear with his hoof.

"YES!!!!!!!" they hollered.

Monty's hat wobbled from side to side. "What's going on up there?" he said, removing the hat.

Hoot, hoot!

A snow white owl, twice the size of his top hat, flapped its wings and soared into the sky.

"Wow!" Rudi said, spellbound.

Monty jiggled and scratched. "Oooh! I'm itchy all over!" he said, cavorting around in circles.

Ronaldo and Rudi were in stitches of laughter. They had seen him do a similar act on television.

"There's something up my sleeve!" Monty unbuttoned it and checked inside.

"Lemmings?!" He whooped.

Two lemmings scurried into his hoof.

"Oooh!" Monty undid the other sleeve.

Two more lemmings popped out.

The audience cheered.

"OOOOOOOOOOOOOH!" Monty's eyes

★ 133 ★

grew as large as carrot and jam scones. "I think there's more!" He wriggled around the garden.

The fawns couldn't stop laughing. Monty unfastened the buttons on his dungarees. The bib dropped. Dozens of lemmings sprung out.

"They'd be nice in a pie," Mrs Sorrenson whispered to Rudi's dad.

Monty took out a deck of cards. "I'm going to need a volunteer," he said in a husky voice. "How about the birthday fawn?"

Rudi rushed up. His scarlet-red magician's cape swung from his shoulders.

Ronaldo looked around. *Where was Vixen?*

Monty shuffled the deck and placed the cards face down on the table.

He turned to his assistant. "Rudi, I want you to think of a card."

"Um... the six of hearts," Rudi said.

"Now, after I touch the cards with my wand, I want you to say the magic word – CARROT-KAZOOO!

"Okay," Rudi nodded with glee.

"One, two three!" The Magician tapped the cards.

"CARROT-KAZOOOOOOOOO!"

Monty turned over the deck and spread out the cards, pictures facing upwards. But in the middle of the deck, one card was face down. Monty pointed to it.

"Rudi, I want you to take that card and show it to the audience," he said.

Rudi pulled the card from the deck and turned it over.

"It's the six of hearts!" He waved it in the air.

The crowd applauded.

"But how did you know?" he said, bamboozled.

"That's magic!" Monty smiled.

Monty continued to impress with one magic trick after another. But by the end of the show, Vixen still hadn't turned up.

The celebrity moose packed up his props and put them in his case.

"Bye, everyone!" He threw his cape over his shoulder with a dramatic flourish, just like he did on his television show. A waft of scent lingered in the air.

Ronaldo wrinkled his nose: lemon and lavender with a hint of peppermint. He had smelt that scent before... that time when he bumped into Vixen!

Ronaldo narrowed his eyes and smiled.

Vixen Pederson had been at the party all along!

Chapter Seventeen

Monty Unmasked

Ronaldo looked around. No one was watching. He sneaked out of the garden and trotted up to the main path. He peered left and right. *Where was Monty the Moose?*

Thump!

Ronaldo rushed in the sounds direction.

Vixen Pederson was sitting beneath a tree, a Monty the Moose mask by his side. Lemmings scurried up and down his legs. He was almost unrecognisable: sweat trickled down his face, and his trademark black quiff was plastered over his forehead.

"Vixen!" Ronaldo folded his arms over his chest and smiled smugly. He must have inherited his mum's detective traits! "I knew it was you!" he said.

"It's so hot under that mask, Ronny," Vixen said. He guzzled from a bottle of carrotade. "I could hardly breathe."

"You were fantastic!"

"How did you know it was me?"

"*Reindeer Roar*!" Ronaldo said, proud of himself.

"D'you think anyone else knows?"

"No." Ronaldo shook his head.

"Then let's keep it that way. We don't

want Rudi thinking he didn't see the real thing."

"But Vixen, how did you know Monty wasn't coming?"

"Monty's my uncle."

"*Your uncle?*" Ronaldo said, flabbergasted.

"Yes. My dad mentioned he wasn't well, so I popped round to see him. When he told me he'd cancelled for Rudi's party, I suggested I do it instead."

"But how do you know all that magic?"

"Uncle Monty's been teaching me tricks since I was young."

"Un-be-lievable," Ronaldo muttered. "You're the best flying reindeer in the world *and* a brilliant magician."

A lemming was attempting to get away. Vixen pounced forward and grabbed it by its tail.

"You'd better get back before anyone notices you're gone," he said and swept his hair from his face. "I need to freshen

up a bit."

Ronaldo dashed back to find Rudi and his parents waving off guests at the gate.

"Thanks, Rudi," Vixie said. "That was the best party I've ever been to."

"You can't go yet!" Ronaldo said. "There's still cake left." He placed a hoof around Vixie's shoulder and ushered her back inside.

Vixie laughed. "Ronny, why are you acting all weird?" she said.

"Just trust me: stay a bit longer."

"Well okay," she said, sneaking a carrot and orange cupcake.

How can I prevent anyone else from

leaving the party? Ronaldo thought, scratching his head. *I know!* He grabbed a tray of strawberry and carrot shortbread and stood in front of the gate. *I'll offfer shortbread to everyone and keep them talking until Vixen arrives.*

"See ya, Ronny," said Rudi's cousins, Donner and Dancy.

Ronaldo blocked them off. "Did you enjoy the Reindeer Flyover?" he asked.

He continued chatting with the cousins about Monty the Moose, and Vixen's workshop, and just as he was about to tell Donner and Dancy about his grandad's skydiving adventure, a gravelly voice rang out.

"HAPPY BIRTHDAY, RUDI!"

Everyone spun around.

Rudi's eyes grew larger than chocolate Wagon-Wheels. Vixen Pederson, the flying hero extraordinaire, was at *his* birthday party.

The celebrity reindeer was mobbed.

"Can I have your autograph?" Vixie said. She shoved a party hat in front of him. "You can write on this."

"Can I have one, too?" Dancy asked.

"I wish you'd come earlier," Rudi said, when he found a quiet moment with Vixen. "Monty the Moose was here."

"Monty the Moose?!" Vixen replied. "I would *love* to have seen him."

With innocent blue eyes, Rudi looked up at Vixen. "Maybe you can book him for your next birthday party?" he suggested.

Vixen caught Ronaldo's eye and winked.

Ronaldo glowed brighter than the floodlights at The Reindeer Flying Academy.

He, Ronaldo the reindeer, shared a special secret with superstar Vixen Pederson!

Chapter Eighteen

Rudi's Birthday Extravaganza

The sky grew dusky. Ronaldo and Rudi's parents, Vixen and Mrs Sorrenson relaxed in armchairs and sipped carrot fizz. Ronaldo and Rudi played *Trump* cards on the floor. Everyone else had gone home.

It had been a terrific day.

"What's in the big box under the table?" Ronaldo's mum asked.

She knew what it was! Amongst all the excitement, Ronaldo had forgotten Rudi's present!

"That's from me!" he said. "I'm such a

scatterbrain." He passed his gift to Rudi. "Happy Birthday!"

Everyone laughed as Rudi ripped off the paper and opened boxes… and ripped off more paper and opened more boxes.

Rudi shook the box. "Is there anything in here?" he giggled.

"You'll have to wait and see," Ronaldo said, snickering.

At last, Rudi was down to the last box. He opened it up.

"*Super* FLY-X!" he shrieked. He yanked the goggles from the box and pulled them over his head. "I *love* the colour!" He hugged his friend. "Thanks, Ronny!"

Ring, ring! Ring, ring!

Mr Gunnersson padded into the hallway to answer the phone.

Rudi stood at the centre of the room, his face glimmering with happiness. "Monty the Moose *and* Vixen Pederson came to my party. I got a new magic kit and *Super FLY-X* goggles. Could my birthday get any more fantastic?"

His dad burst back into the room. "DASHER'S GOT FLU!" he cheered,

dancing around the living room.

"Yes!" Ronaldo jumped up and down with excitement. *A space for Rudi!*

"Ronaldo, that's not very nice," his mum said, frowning.

Mrs Gunnersson gave her husband a disapproving look.

Mr Gunnersson panted with excitement. "When I got the new job," he said, "I tried to reserve a place for Rudi on Vixen's workshop."

Rudi jumped up.

"But it was already full."

"Oh!" Rudi bowed his head.

"That was Wing Commander Blitsen on the phone." Mr Gunnersson shook like a giddy fawn. "Dasher's got the flu! Not that I'm happy he's got flu..."

"No." Ronaldo shook his head in agreement.

"But it leaves one space available on the workshop." Mr Gunnersson stooped down; stared into his son's face.

"Who for?" Rudi asked.

Ronaldo shook his head again. *Oh, Rudi!*

"For you!!!" His dad roared.

"Me?" Rudi's face shone brighter than his luminous lime goggles. "YES!!!!!" He leapt into his dad's arms.

"It's gonna be awesome!" he said bouncing up and down with Ronaldo.

Ronaldo's dad rushed towards the window. "I don't believe it!" he said. "It's snowing!"

"Oh, thank goodness," Ronaldo's mum said. "I'm sick of heat and humidity!"

"I won't have to use that awful *FrizzNo* anymore," Mrs Gunnersson said.

"Yeah, it's really sticky," Ronaldo's dad said in agreement.

"And it gives you dandruff," Mr Gunnersson added.

Ronaldo rolled his eyes. He had finally worked it out. *FrizzNo*! Of course! *That's* what had turned everyone's hair blue!

"Let's go outside, Ronny," Rudi said. "We can build a snowman."

The best pals stormed into the garden.

Vixen followed behind. He crouched down beside them. "There'll be plenty of snow at the workshop," he teased.

"Where's it gonna be?" Ronaldo's dad said, who had been desperate to know.

"Please tell us," Ronaldo begged.

"Pleeease," Rudi said, clasping his hooves under his chin.

"Can you keep a secret?" Vixen asked.

"Yes!"

"Do you promise?"

"YES!!!" Ronaldo's dad said, quivering with excitment.

Vixen paused. He looked around: everyone was waiting.

"It's the North Pole!"

"YEEEEEEEEEEEEEEEEEEEES!!!!!"

The two young reindeer jumped for joy. Ronaldo's dad cart-wheeled around the garden. (Ronaldo had no idea why. Dad wasn't going to the workshop!)

Mr Gunnersson switched on the radio.

"Let's have some music," he said, and he offered a hoof to Mrs Sorrenson. "Care for a dance?"

"I'd be delighted," she replied with a bright smile.

"You'd better be careful!" Mrs Gunnersson laughed. "My husband's got two left hooves!"

Giant snowflakes tumbled from the sky, transforming the garden into a winter wonderland. Ronaldo, Rudi, and Vixen hurled snowballs at each other. Mr Gunnersson twirled Mrs Sorrenson around the sparkling white dance-floor.

"It's a good job Monty the Moose made such a quick recovery," Ronaldo's mum said, sipping her hot chocolate. "And what a wonderful surprise it was to have Vixen turn up, too!"

Mrs Gunnersson wiped blue dye from her face. She smiled as she surveyed the scene in her garden. "Yes, indeed," she said. "Rudi's party turned out to be a real birthday extravaganza!"

Can Ronaldo inspire his team to win the North Pole sleigh race? Find out in his next thrilling adventure, ***Ronaldo: Vixen's Flying Workshop***

getBook.at/my_Amazon4

Message from the Author

Thank you! I very much appreciate you taking the time to read *Ronaldo: Rudi's Birthday Extravaganza*. I hope you enjoyed it and had a few laughs along the way.

I am trying to spread the word about Ronaldo so others can enjoy the fun. As a self-published author, reviews are the best way for me to do this. If you liked the book, please may I ask you to rate it on Amazon, or better still, add a review.

He dreams of winning the North Pole sleigh race. But, his teammate is sure to wreck things!

Santa's top reindeer, Vixen Pederson, is hosting a teamwork workshop—and Ronaldo has his flying goggles packed and ready to go!

In training for a sleigh race, the cadets must work together to win the ultimate prize—Jingle Bells! But Ronaldo's dream turns into a nightmare when Cupid joins his side.

She's the worst flying cadet, ever! And his squabbling teammates are plotting to put her out of the race.

But Cupid isn't who she appears to be. And when Ronaldo discovers she is the granddaughter of a world famous flying champion, he suspects she is guarding a secret. And the only way to lead his team to victory—is to find out what it is.

Buy ***Ronaldo: Vixen's Flying Workshop*** and race to the finish line today!

getBook.at/my_Amazon4

Catch a sneak peek of
Ronaldo: Vixen's Flying Workshop

Ronaldo rummaged under the bed. *Where were they?*

The bedroom door flew open and his dad stomped into the room. "I'm so excited! I haven't slept a wink."

He stumbled over Ronaldo's back hooves and sloshed half a mug of steaming hot chocolate over the rug.

Ronaldo crawled out from under the bed.

"But you're not going to the North Pole, Dad – *I* am!" He twirled a pair of cherry-red flying goggles in the air, quivering from antler to tail.

"I can't wait to see Vixen Pederson again!" Ronaldo said.

He gazed at the poster of his hero plastered on the wall, a golden Jingle Bell glinting around his thick, raven-black collar.

"I'm gonna fly out of my fur to impress him."

Ronaldo grabbed the mug from his dad and sat on the bed beside him.

"I wonder if Santa will be there," Dad said, staring into space. "I've wanted to meet him my *whole* life."

"There's Carrot Flakes in the kitchen!" Mum hollered from downstairs.

Dad jumped up from the bed. The sudden bounce took Ronaldo by surprise and he slopped the rest of his drink over the covers.

When the spillage had been mopped up, Ronaldo brushed and flossed his teeth, combed the knots out of his fur, and polished his antlers with Reindeer Glow, a new wax advertised on the TV. Finally, he pulled on leggings, his best Aran-knit jumper, and hurried downstairs.

"Have you packed your flying goggles?" Mum asked.

"Yep," Ronaldo answered, sitting down at the kitchen table.

"And a spare set?"

Ronaldo nodded. He had packed a spare set for the spare set... and the red set just in case.

He sprinkled a teaspoon of sugar over his cereal. Mum whipped the sugar bowl away before he had the chance to take anymore.

"You must be so excited," she said.

"I am!" Dad replied.

"Not you! Ronaldo!"

"I am ex-thited!" Ronaldo said with his mouth full of Carrot Flakes. He paused to wipe milk off his chin. "But I suppose I'm a bit nervous, too."

"Nervous? You're the top Flying Cadet at

the Reindeer Flying Academy!"

"But it's a teamwork workshop, Mum, and I've never flown in a group."

"Well, you'll be learning from Santa's team! They're the best flyers in the world."

"Let's go," Dad called from the hallway. He held his son's red flying jacket out for him. Ronaldo slipped his arms through the sleeves and pulled on his hat.

"Have a fabulous time," Mum said, hugging him. "And don't go wandering anywhere on your own."

"Yes, the North Pole is FULL of dangerous animals," Dad added.

Mum gave him a hard stare.

"I promise I'll stay with the school group," Ronaldo said. He kissed his mum on the cheek and waved goodbye.

The early morning sky was black as liquorice. But fresh snow made the woods appear brighter. Father and son trudged towards the Meeting Point. The crunching of their hooves and the hoot of a distant owl were the only sounds in the otherwise silent forest.

An orange light glimmered up ahead.

"What's that?" Dad asked, squinting.

"Rudi's new leggings," Ronaldo chuckled. "They glow in the dark."

Ronaldo's best friend was waiting with his dad.

"I've been awake all night," Rudi said with eyes as huge as plum puddings. "I'm so excited I think I'm going to explode!"

The young reindeer jabbered on together as they trekked towards the flying school.

"I wonder how we're getting to the North Pole," Rudi said.

The travel plans were top-secret! And not knowing had been driving them bananas. Ronaldo knew his parents had signed a consent form, but every time he searched for it, his mum had appeared.

"I reckon it's the *Polar Express* train," Ronaldo said.

"I hope we go by plane!"

"Ooh, me too! I've never been on an aeroplane."

The group approached the Reindeer Flying Academy: the most famous flying school in the world.

They spotted something!

"ELVES!!!" Rudi squealed.

"Shussh," his dad scolded. "And don't point. It's rude."

"Sorry," Rudi whispered.

The group tottered towards Wing Commander Blitsen, Ronaldo and Rudi's superior officer.

"Are you looking forward to the

workshop?" she asked, sweeping her white hair from her face. "It's such a marvellous opportunity. *Marvellous!*"

She introduced an elf no taller than the cadets. "This is Gordy," she announced. "I'm leaving you in his tiny but capable hands."

Ronaldo had seen pictures of elves in fairytale books, but none of them had bubblegum-pink hair like Gordy. The colour reminded him of a strawberry cupcake he'd once eaten.

"Can I have your names, please?" the elf asked in a high-pitched voice.

"Rudolph Gunnersson."

The little man ticked the name off his list.

"I'm Ronaldo."

"Ronaldo? Aren't reindeer usually named Donner, Vixen, Dancer, Cupid, Dasher,

Prancer, Rudolph, Comet or Blitsen?"

"Yes, he's the only one!" Dad interrupted. "I named him after my favourite footballer," he said proudly.

Ronaldo often wished he hadn't! He'd been teased by other cadets because of his name.

"Well, I think it's splendid," the elf replied, "nobody will ever forget who you are." He lowered his list and smiled. "Please make your way to runway four... your *vehicle* awaits you."

"Yippee!" the two cadets whooped with delight.

Not wanting to wait a second longer, they hugged their dads goodbye, and charged like soldiers onto a battlefield. "We're going by plane!" they shrieked.

Gordy watched on, with a confused expression. There was no aeroplane on runway four!

How will Ronaldo and Rudi get to the North Pole? Find out now in, *Ronaldo: Vixen's Flying Workshop*

getBook.at/my_Amazon4

Printed in Great Britain
by Amazon

18162886R00098